BIG WORLD, SMALL WORLD

Jeanne Titherington

Greenwillow Books, New York

Library of Congress Cataloging in Publication Data

Titherington, Jeanne.
Big world, small world.
Summary: Though they spend the day doing things
together, Anna and her mother see the same
things in very different ways.
[1. Mothers and daughters—Fiction] I. Title.
PZ7.T53Bi 1985   [E]   84-4140
ISBN 0-688-04022-5
ISBN 0-688-04023-3 (lib. bdg.)

To my Mother and Auntie Pri

"Verily I say unto you, Whosoever shall not
receive the kingdom of God as a little child,
he shall not enter therein."

—MARK 10:15

It's Saturday morning.
Mama gets up.

Anna gets up too.

Mama checks her face
in the mirror.

Anna checks her toes.

Mama puts on her clothes.

Anna puts on Mama's shoes.

Mama drinks her coffee.

Anna drinks her milk.

Mama carries her pocketbook.

Anna carries her teddy.

Mama watches traffic lights.

Anna watches Mama's feet.

Mama looks for what she needs.

Anna looks for what she likes.

Mama counts her money.

Anna counts people's legs.

Mama talks to a neighbor.

Anna talks to his dog.

Home again.
Mama gets a kiss.

Anna gives a hug.

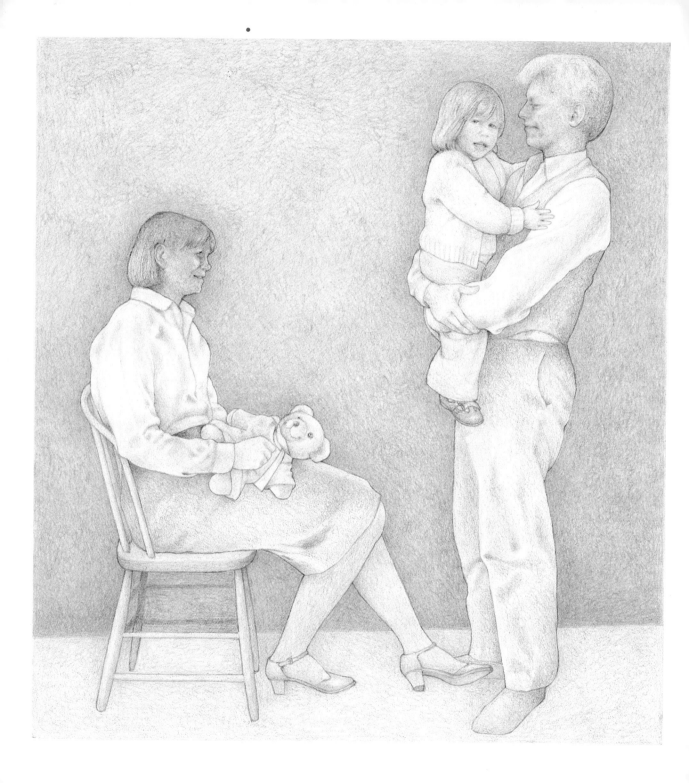